Sweet Polly Petals

John Gray & Shanna Brickell

author and illustrator of
Keller's Heart

PARACLETE PRESS
Brewster, Massachusetts

Sweet Polly Petals

2020 First Printing

Sweet Polly Petals

Text copyright © 2020 by John Gray

Illustrations copyright © 2020 by Shanna Obelenus

ISBN 978-1-64060-555-8

The Paraclete Press name and logo (dove on cross) are trademarks of
Paraclete Press, Inc.

Library of Congress Cataloging-in-Publication Data
Names: Gray, John Joseph, 1962- author. | Brickell, Shanna, illustrator.
Title: Sweet Polly Petals / by John Gray ; illustrated by Shanna Brickell.
Description: Brewster, Massachusetts : Paraclete Press, 2020. | Audience:
    Grades 2-3. | Summary: "A little magic grants Polly's wishes to help
    others"— Provided by publisher.
Identifiers: LCCN 2019057065 (print) | LCCN 2019057066 (ebook) | ISBN
    9781640605558 (hardcover) | ISBN 9781640605565 (epub) | ISBN
    9781640605572 (pdf)
Subjects: CYAC: Wishes—Fiction. | Homeless persons—Fiction. |
    Kindness—Fiction.
Classification: LCC PZ7.1.G733 Sw 2020 (print) | LCC PZ7.1.G733 (ebook) |
    DDC [E]—dc23
LC record available at https://lccn.loc.gov/2019057065
LC ebook record available at https://lccn.loc.gov/2019057066

10 9 8 7 6 5 4 3 2 1

Published by Paraclete Press
Brewster, Massachusetts
www.paracletepress.com

Manufactured by Regent Publishing Services Limited, Hong Kong
Printed June, 2020, in ShenZhen, Guangdong, China

For every kind soul who
has dedicated their life to helping the less fortunate
and easing the world's suffering.

*T*here once was a town, just like yours, with a girl named Sweet Polly Petals. Everyone called her that because of a flower, a wish, and a little bit of magic.

Pancakes and rainbows, jelly beans and butterfly kisses—Polly had lots of favorite things. But nothing made her happier than playing in the park.

It had a bright yellow swing, a pond with silly ducks and tall trees, perfect to have a picnic under. There were also benches to sit on, although sometimes Polly saw people sleeping on them. *How strange,* she thought, *People usually sleep on beds.*

"Who are they?" she asked her mom. After a thoughtful pause her mother said, "Just regular people who lost their way, sweetheart." Polly responded innocently, "Can we help them find it again? Do they need a map?" Her mom hugged her and said, "No, dear, mostly they need food, a home, someone to care."

A few days later Polly and her mom were back at the park for a picnic, and on the bench she noticed a woman she'd seen before. The woman wore a baggy coat and was always holding a potted flower. As her mom spread the blanket under a tree, Polly walked over with her peanut butter sandwich and a bottle of water.

"Hi, I'm Polly," she began, "You hungry? I don't mind sharing." The woman smiled warmly and said, "Thank you, hon, I'm not hungry, but my flower is thirsty." It was a beautiful purple orchid. Polly poured her water into the pot, and the petals on the orchid seemed to glow with delight.

The woman then said, "Do you believe in magic? I ask because this is a magic orchid." Polly scratched her head and said, "It just looks like a regular flower to me."

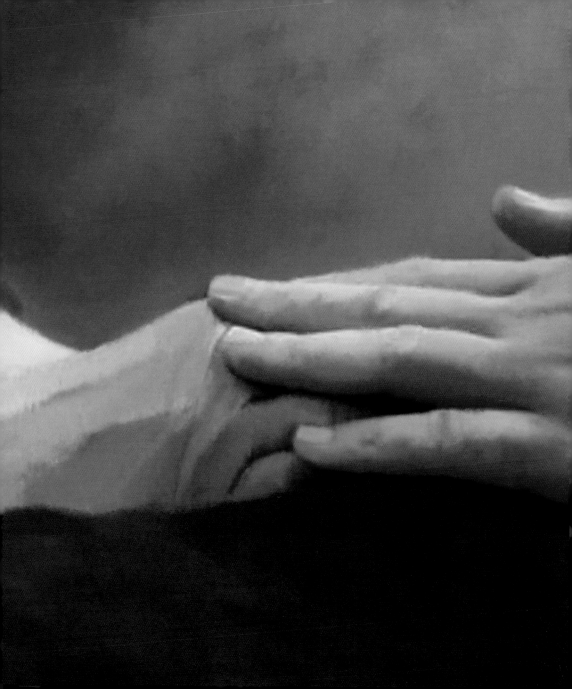

The woman then explained, "This orchid can grant wishes. But there are two things to understand. First, you can't ask for anything for yourself." Polly thought for a second and said, "So you have to help other people with your wish?" "That's right," she responded, "and the second thing is, every time a wish is granted the flower loses a petal."

Polly could see there were only four petals left. "So, four wishes?" she asked. "That's right, just four left," the woman said. "Here, I want you to have it. Just remember what I said."

Holding the flower, Polly returned to her mom and shared the story about the orchid. She could tell her mother was doubtful, so, "Let's test it out," Polly said. "I wish all the people in this park would get a sweet treat right now."

Just then they heard the music of
an ice cream truck approaching. The
man pulled into the park and told
everyone that his freezer was broken
and everything was melting, so if anyone
wanted free ice cream, they could have it.

Polly looked at the orchid, and a single
purple petal fell to the soft grass. She
scooped it up and put it in her pocket.

Walking home with her mom she saw a woman standing next to a car with a flat tire. She looked so upset. Polly felt bad so she said out loud, "I wish that woman had help."

Just then a police officer drove by, saw the woman, and got out to change her tire. Another petal from the orchid fell to the ground and Polly placed it gently in her pocket.

When they returned home, she saw the boy next door was crying. "What's wrong, Tommy?" she asked. "I left the gate open and my dog Eli ran away," he said. Polly looked at her mom and down at the orchid. There were only two petals left. "Should I?" she asked. "It's up to you, sweetie," her mom replied.

Polly put her hand on Tommy's shoulder and said, "It's going to be all right. I wish Eli would come home." Just then they heard the phone ringing in the house. Tommy's mom answered and told everyone a kind stranger had found Eli a mile away and he was safe. Polly put her hand out and caught the third petal as it fell.

That night Polly sat on her bed and stared at the last petal on the orchid, wondering what should be her last wish? The next morning, she knew.

Polly went back to the park and found the woman on the bench. She handed her the orchid with one petal remaining and said, "My final wish is to help you. I want you to have a home." The woman's eyes filled with tears because of Polly's kindness. Just then the last petal fell into Polly's tiny hand, and she smiled because she knew the woman in the park would be okay.

"There's one last thing you need to do," the woman said to Polly. "Take the petals in your pocket and plant them in your yard. Only this time I want you to make a wish for yourself. Something big and important." Polly buried the petals as she was told and went to sleep.

The next morning, when she woke, her yard was filled with hundreds of bright purple orchids. Somehow, like magic, they had grown overnight. The little girl's big wish was to continue granting wishes. And now the child they called Sweet Polly Petals had enough petals to help everyone.

About the Author

John Gray is an Emmy Award-winning writer of two popular children's books who has published thousands of columns and short stories. His books, *God Needed a Puppy* and *Keller's Heart*, have been number-one bestsellers in several categories on Amazon.com and have been purchased by families in all 50 US states and numerous other countries.

His stories always have a well-grounded moral center, seeking to teach children that kindness is the path to happiness.

He donates a generous portion of book sales to help others, including giving $30,000 to more than 50 animal shelters around the country.

John is a father of three who lives in upstate New York with his wife, Courtney, and their five dogs, three of which are rescues with special needs.

John plans to use a portion of the proceeds from this new children's book, *Sweet Polly Petals*, to help the homeless.

About the Illustrator

As a child I was in awe of what could be created with a box of crayons and a few sheets of paper. This mystery and magic still inspires me. My mission for each of my paintings is to capture, image by image, the beauty in all that is around us, and to infuse my artwork with energy and light that connect with each viewer's heart.

You may also enjoy these beautiful books from
John Gray and Shanna Brickell...

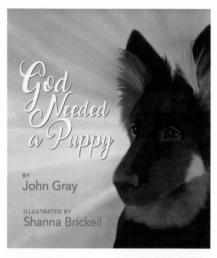

God Needed a Puppy

ISBN 978-1-64060-148-2 | Hardcover | $12.99

Edgar the Owl and Freddy the
Fox show readers of all ages how
saying goodbye to a beloved
animal does not mean saying
goodbye forever.

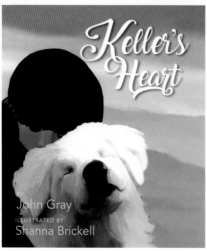

Keller's Heart

ISBN 978-1-64060-174-1 | Hardcover | $12.99

Two friends teach the world to
see people by the only thing that
really matters ... the heart.

Available at bookstores
Paraclete Press | 1-800-451-5006 | www.paracletepress.com

A Note from the Author

I once met a man in a homeless shelter and asked him what he needed most. I assumed he'd say food, warm clothes, or a safe place to sleep. Instead he simply said, "I want to be seen." His words were as haunting as they were sad.

Years later, I sat down to write a story, and the image of a little girl holding a purple orchid appeared in my head. I tried to push away the vision but she was persistent. Every day for a week when I tried to write anything, the same child appeared in my conscience, blocking the way, demanding I tell her story.

Soon after, while sitting at a traffic light, I noticed a homeless man in tattered clothes, holding a sign, asking for help. All the motorists looked right through him like he wasn't there. As I handed him spare change through the car window, I remembered the words from the man in the shelter, and for some reason my mind turned to that little girl with the purple flowers. That evening I sat down and wrote this story.

It is a hard world, and we all need help sometimes. And no one should be invisible. By purchasing this book, you are showing a kindness to the homeless, as a portion of the proceeds will be donated to help them.

Thank you,

John Gray